RULES OF SUMMER

Shaun Tan

LOTHIAN
Children's Books

For the little and the big.

A Lothian Children's Book
Published in Australia and New Zealand in 2013
by Hachette Australia
Level 17, 207 Kent Street, Sydney NSW 2000
www.hachettechildrens.com.au
www.shauntan.net

5 7 9 10 8 6 4

Text and illustrations copyright © Shaun Tan 2013

National Library of Australia
Cataloguing-in-Publication data:

Tan, Shaun, author.

Rules of summer / Shaun Tan.

978 0 7344 1067 2 (hardback).

A823.3

Designed by Shaun Tan
Art photography by Matthew Stanton
Colour reproduction by Hell Colour Australia
Printed in China by Toppan Leefung Printing Limited

Many thanks to Helen Chamberlin, Tegan Morrison, Jon Appleton, Suzanne O'Sullivan
and the Hachette team, Sophie Byrne, Inari Kiuru, Will Lauria, Julia Adams, Melbourne
Artists' Supplies, Australian Society of Authors, Klaus Humann and Arthur Levine.

A *RULES OF SUMMER*
APP IS ALSO AVAILABLE
WeAreWheelbarrow.com

This is what I learned last summer:

Never leave a red sock on the clothesline.

Never eat the last olive at a party.

Never drop your jar.

Never leave the back door open overnight.

Never step on a snail.

Never be late for a parade.

Never ruin a perfect plan.

Never argue with an umpire.

Never give your keys to a stranger.

Never forget the password.

Never ask for a reason.

Never lose a fight.

Never wait for an apology.

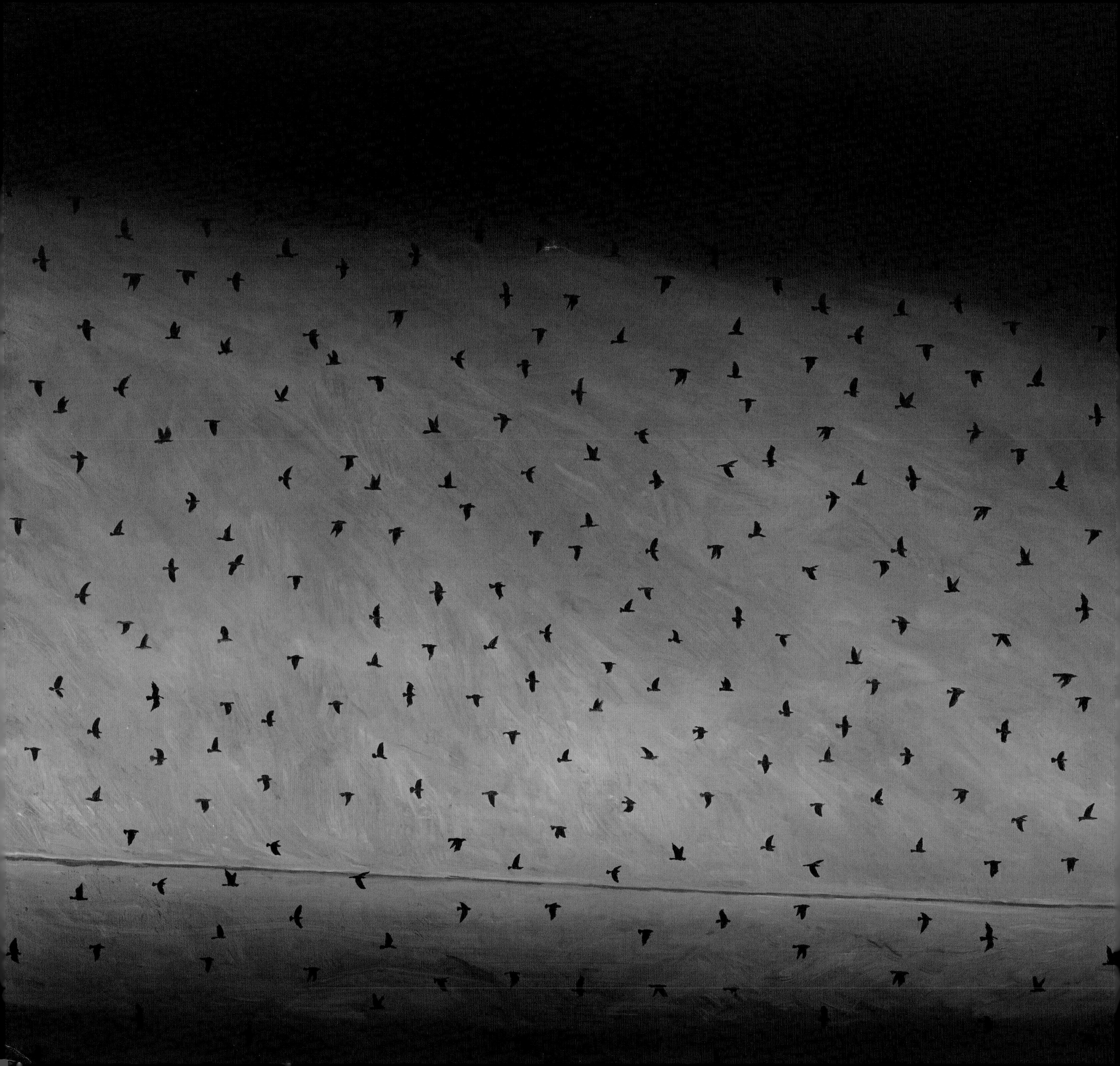

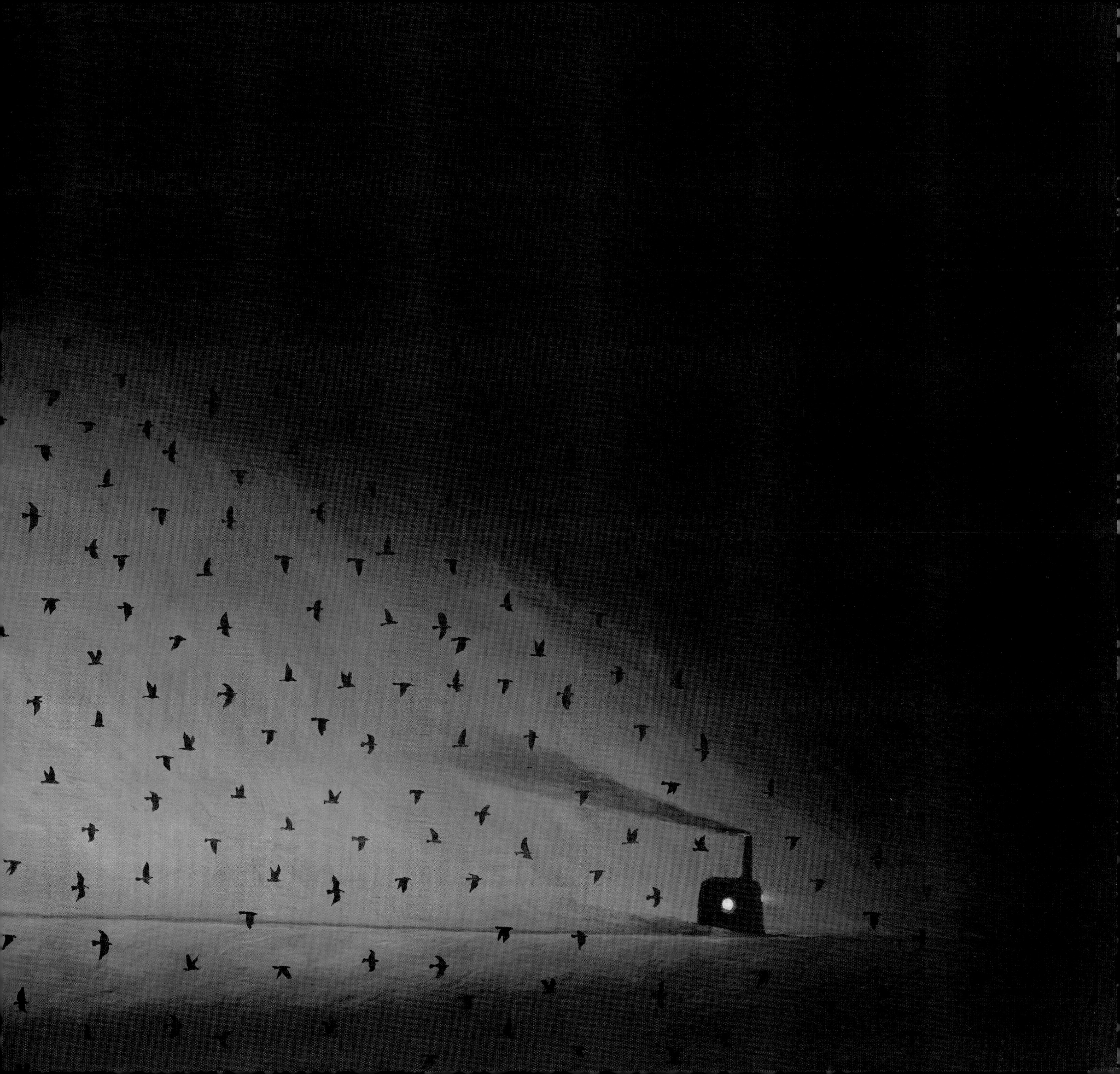

Always bring bolt cutters.

Always know the way home.

Never miss the last day of summer.

That's it.